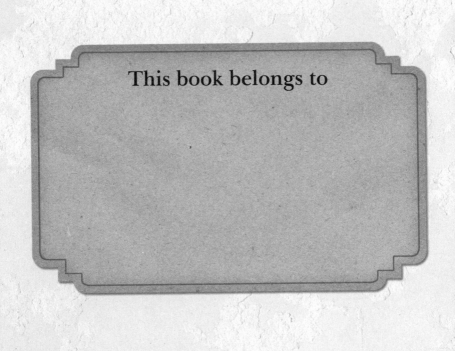

This book belongs to

A Descendants Scrapbook
Isle of the Lost Edition

Mal

Jay

Carlos

Evie

AND UMA!

studio fun
INTERNATIONAL

WELCOME to Our Scrapbook!

Coming to Auradon turned our lives upside down—and then we chose to stay here! There have been barely believable stories and unforgettable discoveries. So, we decided to put our memories down in one place.

Ta-da! Our scrapbook! We to all the photos from our recer adventures and put them all together, with notes to make sure we never forget the amazing times we've had.

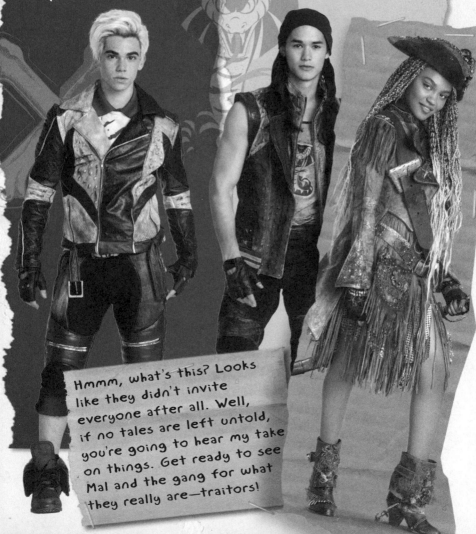

Think we've been sitting around Auradon? Going to class? Guess again. It's been a whirlwind. Back to the Isle of the Lost twice! Magic spells backfired and royalty was kidnapped. And oh yeah, my dog started talking like a person.

And that's not even the weirdest thing that's happened. Just ask our friends, they're in here too! Our stories wouldn't be complete without them, so we invited them to join in! Get ready to hear all the details—no tales left untold.

Hmmm, what's this? Looks like they didn't invite everyone after all. Well, if no tales are left untold, you're going to hear my take on things. Get ready to see Mal and the gang for what they really are—traitors!

Auradon Here We Come

If we look kinda like a gang, that's because we <u>were</u> kinda like a gang. Our turf stretched from one crummy corner of the Isle of the Lost to the other.

Sure, it's lame to blame your parents for behaving badly. But here, the parents in question are literally evil. Scheming isn't just their favorite hobby—it's their lives!

One day, Ben—still "just" a prince—got all big-hearted and invited us to school in Auradon. We quickly found out that not everyone—like his girlfriend Audrey—was so excited to host us. I took care of her, and I don't mean I made her chicken soup.

They thought a private class in being good taught by Fairy Godmother (might as well be Fairy Goodmother) would set us straight. Want to see how well that worked?

Yeah, I'm not sure it's working. Maybe they thought they were in gym class? It'd be a little weird to hold gym in the library. But there was plenty of weird things happening—for one, we were starting to like Auradon.

For Carlos, it was meeting Dude. His mom had made him fear dogs. Then he realized she is a lot scarier than Dude ever was.

Evie discovered that instead of being into castles and princes, she was actually into chemistry and trumpet players. And was Doug ever into her, too!

Jay found out that he loved ... being loved. Seriously, by almost every girl in school. And when he turned out to be a sports star too, he wouldn't even leave for a magic lamp.

And then there's me. It's pretty simple, really—I realized I liked Ben. At least, a lot more than I liked helping my mother in an evil plot to steal Fairy Godmother's wand. So, maybe it's not that simple after all! Point is, I was happy to stay. At least I thought I was ...

Mal

I used to rob candy from babies. What can I say? Like mother, like daughter—at least, while I was growing up. Thankfully that's not true anymore, because if it were I'd be a lizard.

Coming to Auradon changed me. I discovered that the people I'd hated my whole life were just . . . people, and some of them were amazing! Like Ben. Meeting him, realizing I wasn't like my mother, standing up to her . . . it all felt so good.

Me and mom, before she grew a tail. Again.

She always pretended to be the victim, but guess who really was? Me!

The old me.

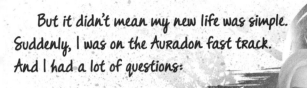

But it didn't mean my new life was simple. Suddenly, I was on the Auradon fast track. And I had a lot of questions:

Can I really leave the Isle behind?

Queen? Me? Yeah, no.

Does Ben really care about me?

Girl, they're called colors. Where they at?

Neat on the outside, inside: total mess.

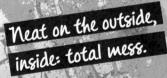

What a phony! OF COURSE she can't leave the Isle behind! She NEVER will. She was BORN there.

Where We Live

Mal

Here's the room Evie and I share at school. It's where we hang out, study, and plot villainous schemes—just kidding (sort of)! It's pretty classic Auradon style—kinda princessy—but we've done our best to make it our own. Let me tell you, the bed is waaaay more comfortable than what I was sleeping on back on the Isle. I'm not even going to call that a bed; it was as soft as a shipping crate.

DON'T FEED MY MOM!

Technically, we've got a third roommate, but she doesn't take up much space. Before I made this sign, you should see what Jay would toss in there. Sometimes it wasn't even food, she'd still eat it.

While Mal's cleaning up after her mom, I'm on my side, coming up with new fashion designs. For me, our room is as much a studio as a bedroom. Big advantage: When I work late, the commute to bed takes 1.5 seconds.

Evie

When I sketch new pieces, suddenly we have new posters. Mal's pretty tolerant of seeing my drawings everywhere. It works for her, though—she's my number one model!

Satin sheets? You know what we use? Fishing nets. Tough girls don't sleep in princess beds.

Evie

Do you think the most important thing in life is looking pretty so that a rich prince will look after you? Wrong! It took me a little while to figure that out, though. Blame my mom, the Evil Queen, for making me looks-obsessed—she kinda has a thing for mirrors. In Auradon, sure, I found my prince. I thought he liked me too, but it turned out he just liked me doing his homework. I moved on fast, and never looked back—there's so much opportunity in Auradon, everyone should have a chance to live here!

This outfit is one of my first creations!

Who's the fairest of them all? Mom had a lot to say about that. Me? Not so much.

After the Coronation, my career was really taking off—and I was still in school! It was a dream come true, and I was about to take on my biggest project yet: designing for the Cotillion.

Oh, your dreams came true? I'm so happy for you.

Like my outfit? I made it myself!

The Cotillion is Coming!

If you were surrounded by this many people on the Isle of the Lost, it meant you were being mobbed. In Auradon, it means you are holding a press conference.

Ben showed up to take some of the heat, right in the nick of time. He deals with this official thing so naturally, I felt like I'd never be good at it.

Yeah, he's pretty cute. But is this true love?

Evie's fittings run on a tight schedule, and it was my turn. The clock was ticking, and it's not like I needed to squeeze into some impossibly tight gown or anything.

Sure, looks great.

Try breathing in it though.

Evie did an amazing job, but something didn't feel right. It was like bit by bit, everything I recognized about myself just disappeared, replaced by an icy blonde doll. Yikes!

BEN

It's tough to be normal when everyone says "Prince" before your name, and people treat your birthday like it's a national holiday. Luckily, I have Belle and Beast for parents—not your typical queen and king.

Bringing Mal and her friends to Auradon is my proudest accomplishment, partly because it taught me to expect the unexpected. Heck, when your girlfriend's mother can turn into a dragon, you better look out.

Trying to look calm under ROYAL pressure for my first royal portrait. Am I pulling it off?

So yeah, my mom used to talk to furniture, and my dad's old shampoo bill would bankrupt a small country.

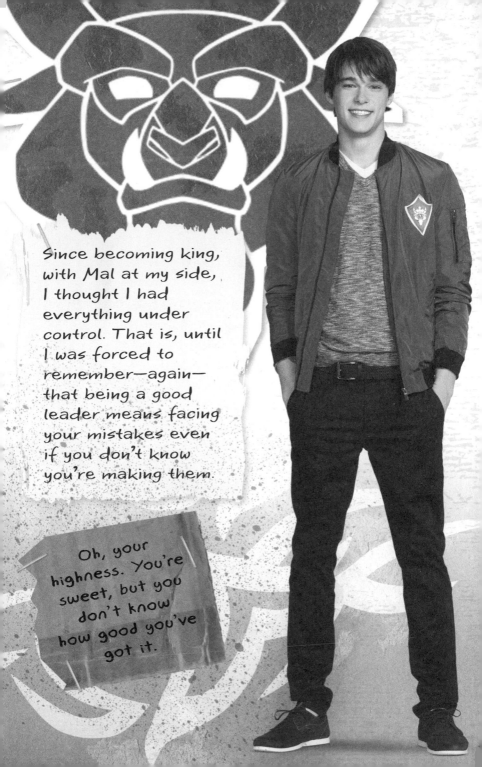

Since becoming king, with Mal at my side, I thought I had everything under control. That is, until I was forced to remember—again—that being a good leader means facing your mistakes even if you don't know you're making them.

Oh, your highness. You're sweet, but you don't know how good you've got it.

Yup. If ol' King Ben had decided to invite me and my friends to Auradon, instead of Mal and hers, who knows what could've happened between me and Ben. Funny thing is, Mal and I used to be friends. But then we grew apart, starting maybe at the exact moment she dumped a bucket of rotting shrimps on my head. Seems a silly thing now, but we were young.

When you live on different ends of the Isle, you find ways to avoid each other. She had Evie, Carlos, and Jay, and I had Gil and Harry—and they're all I need.

Gil   Me   Harry

TROUBLE IS HERE

So, some basics: I'm Uma, my mom is Ursula. Some people call her a sea witch, but to me she's just an independent businessperson who happens to use magic. She brought me up the same way. Not that I like what I do or anything, but being forced to stay on the Isle left me with how many options? Exactly one. On a good day.

Think I sound bitter?

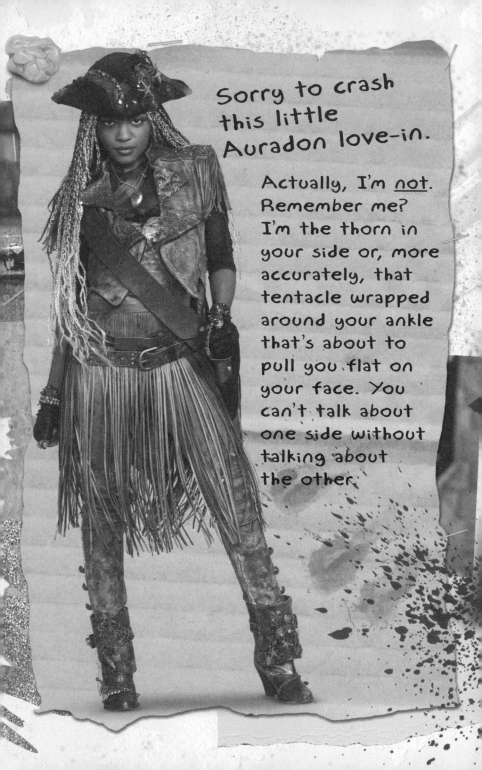

Sorry to crash this little Auradon love-in.

Actually, I'm <u>not</u>. Remember me? I'm the thorn in your side or, more accurately, that tentacle wrapped around your ankle that's about to pull you flat on your face. You can't talk about one side without talking about the other.

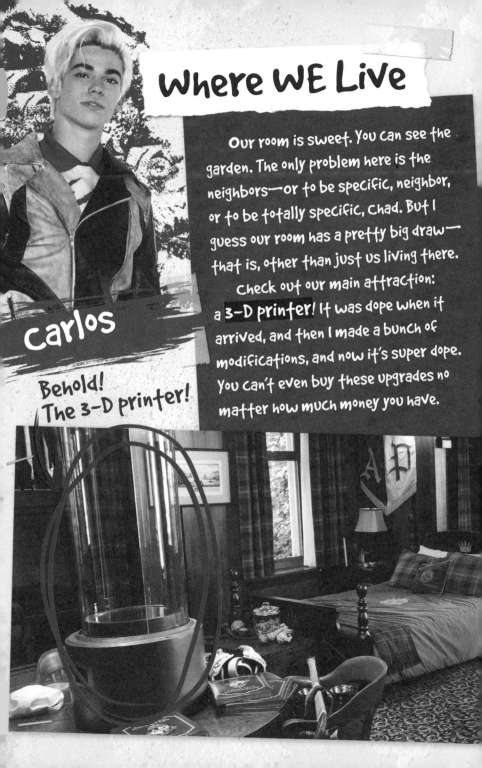

Where WE Live

Our room is sweet. You can see the garden. The only problem here is the neighbors—or to be specific, neighbor, or to be totally specific, Chad. But I guess our room has a pretty big draw—that is, other than just us living there.

Check out our main attraction: a 3-D printer! It was dope when it arrived, and then I made a bunch of modifications, and now it's super dope. You can't even buy these upgrades no matter how much money you have.

Carlos

Behold!
The 3-D printer!

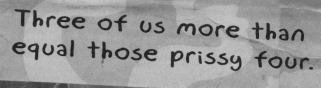

Three of us more than equal those prissy four.

Then Ben made his big proclamation. Great idea in principle, unless you are the one being left behind.

I watched Mal get everything I ever wanted through the static of our busted television. If I ever had a chance to settle the score, I told myself, I'd do it—

no matter what!

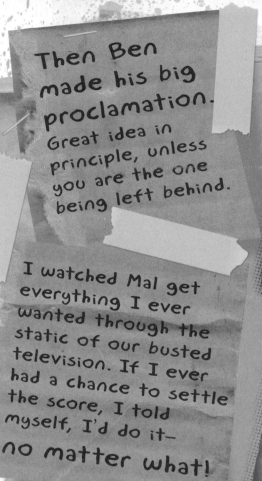

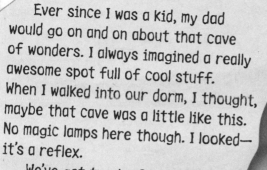

Ever since I was a kid, my dad would go on and on about that cave of wonders. I always imagined a really awesome spot full of cool stuff. When I walked into our dorm, I thought, maybe that cave was a little like this. No magic lamps here though. I looked—it's a reflex.

We've got trunks for keeping stuff secure. On the Isle, people used trash cans for that. Trust me, a trunk is better. You're less likely to open it and find apple cores and fish heads on top of your gear.

Jay

I get it. You guys left the Isle and got...totally boring.

Carlos

Back on the Isle, I was brought up in a pretty weird atmosphere. I thought all dogs were monsters, and that it was normal when your mom made you scrape her bunions. Ugh. Those bunions—they were the real monsters.

Auradon wasn't what I expected. The dog I met didn't want to eat me. He just wanted a friend, which I generally prefer to being eaten. I wondered how to look after him, but then I just took how my mom treated me and did the opposite. It worked out great, plus I'm not sure he'd be too good at scraping bunions.

Me and Mom

Back then, I had a serious attitude problem.

Matching outfits with your dog is SO cool. Wait, it's not. He just loves you because you feed him. BURN!

TAKE THAT, MOM! I'M A DOG LOVER!

After we decided to stay, I started settling in to my new life in Auradon. With all the romance around me, I started to feel a little left out. I had my eye on someone, but could I tell her how I felt?

JAY

My dad is Jafar, and he raised me to be a thief. It made me kind of a loner, I guess. That was fine because then I only had to split the loot one way—mine. I eventually made friends with Mal, Evie, and Carlos, and realized there was more to life than helping my dad find a magic lamp he was never going to track down.

When I first arrived in Auradon, all I could think about were all the things I could steal. And let me tell you, there was a ton! But when I started playing Tourney for the school team, I found something more valuable: sharing a victory with my teammates.

WHAT RULES MORE—

X TOURNEY

✓ OR ME?

Bet I know your answer...

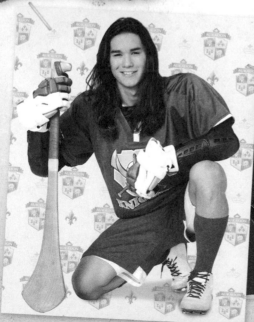

Tourney photo! Pretty hot for a cool guy, right?

Wonder what Dad is scheming...

Still the hottest.

Recently, I became captain of the R.O.A.R. team. It taught me my next lesson in being a good team player: The most important thing about a team is having the right people on it—even if it means getting creative with the rules.

Think you impress all the girls? Well <u>not this one</u>.

Your dad was a <u>villain</u>, Jay. You're just a jock.

Lonnie

My mom's not a mighty queen or evil sorceress. Nope, she's just a famous warrior and overall military genius who struggled against oppression to defend her family. I don't mean to brag, but she's kind of a hero, and not just to me.

I always liked living in Auradon, but it can get a bit stuffy. Not exactly a ton of fashion options to choose from, and I was on the lookout for something fresh. Sure, it's not overthrowing an empire, but when it comes to self-expression every victory counts. So when Mal and the gang showed up with their rebel Isle style, I signed up faster than Chad at an autograph session—that's if he ever got asked.

Looking sassy, plus I spent less on product.

Then, I started following in my mom's footsteps. I decided to train my warrior instincts—starting with my fencing. I thought practicing with others who shared my passion would be easy, but it turned into my own fight against oppression.

used to say I'd never been

to the Isle of the Lost.

I can't say that anymore.

Let's R.O.A.R.

Auradon has tons of awesome sports. Well, at least two. There's Tourney, and there's R.O.A.R, which has the advantage of being named after yelling! Just kidding—it stands for Royal Order Auradon Regiment, and it demands some pretty serious skill, because you might end up with a sword stuck somewhere you don't want it.

Here's the arena before a practice. We duel around the obstacles using fencing rapiers.

Our team is called the Auradon Knights.
Check out these awesome banners!

Funny thing is, if you told me back on the Isle of the Lost that I'd ever be something called a knight, I'd have laughed in your face. But I guess there's a little bit of a hero in here somewhere.

Know who isn't a hero? Chad. Lonnie, who is a killer fencer, wanted to join the team. Here, Chad is quoting some ancient rule about a team being a captain and eight men. Can you say, "Buzzkill"? Lonnie is ten times the fighter Chad is. I knew I had to find a way to get her on the team!

Chad

Did I hear my name? Some people say "charming is as charming does", but better people say "charming is whoever is named charming, peasant." I might not be king—yet—but I've certainly proven myself as Auradon's spiritual leader. If you're seeking enlightenment, just bask in my glow. Heads up: You might have to fight your way through a crowd.

Audrey, my alabaster sculpture, why did you forsake me? I'm waiting for your call, day or night.

Not a drop of that rotten Isle in this blue blood.

Pure Auradon, born and bred.

With this much responsibility, you're wondering how I make time for studying, right? Well, that's where I turn to the support of the community. For a while, Evie understood her role in my grand scheme, but then she really fell out of the picture. WHO CARES?! Audrey asked me to the Coronation. Princesses and Princes—just as it should be.

EVIE'S 4 HEARTS

For me, fashion isn't about blending in.

It's about expressing who you are on the inside.

When my designs started taking off, I decided to start my first business:

Evie's 4 Hearts.

Of course, it's also named after the four of us coming to Auradon together. I couldn't have done this without having amazing friends to be inspired by.

Not every client is a keeper, though. While some of them want to collaborate and explore, some come in with their own vision. Can you guess who I mean? That's right.

I'm not sure which Chad likes more, pretending to be king, or having people waiting on him. Luckily, I've found someone better to "work" with.

Doug's been totally amazing and supportive and has really helped me keep on top of my income. I can't think of anyone I'd prefer to fantasize with about how to spend it!

That bow tie makes me squeal!

Just when I thought it couldn't get dorkier.

DOUG

Hi, uh, ho—Dopey's son here. You hear of personal branding? It's where people make their name stand for something. Try doing that with a name like "Dopey." I love my dad, but I've fought the family name all the way, trying to be involved and cool as possible—you know, like, by being in the band.

Seriously, band is cool. Think Evie would be my girlfriend if it wasn't? Actually, she probably would—that's how cool she is. When I met her, you could have called me son of Bashful. Incredibly, she realized she liked me instead of Chad. This was after she realized he was a jerk.

I mean, I get the curb appeal—would you go for son of Charming, or son of Dopey?

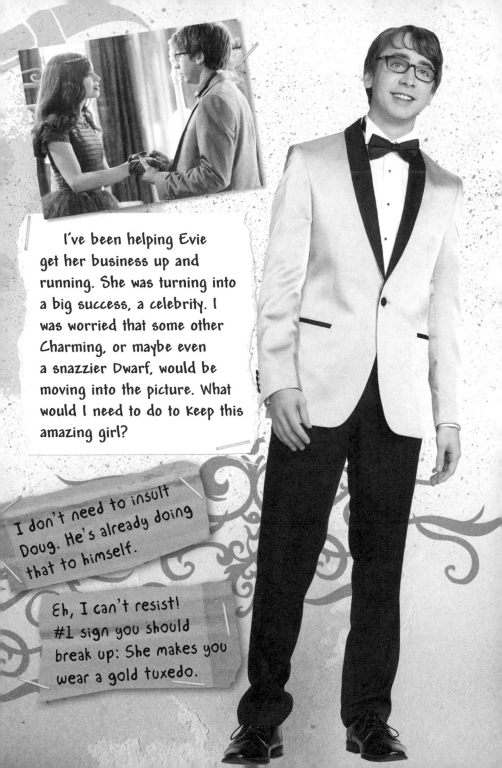

I've been helping Evie get her business up and running. She was turning into a big success, a celebrity. I was worried that some other Charming, or maybe even a snazzier Dwarf, would be moving into the picture. What would I need to do to keep this amazing girl?

I don't need to insult Doug. He's already doing that to himself.

Eh, I can't resist! #1 sign you should break up: She makes you wear a gold tuxedo.

The Fashionista and

The Villain and

Evie & Doug

People talk about having chemistry, like it's romantic, but they generally don't fall for each other in an actual chemistry class.

It helped that you're actually really terrific at chemistry.

Not that I knew that to begin with! I was raised to think all I was good for was being pretty. It's tough not to trust your mom, especially if her name is literally "Evil Queen."

Lucky for both of us, what someone is called doesn't always say everything about a person. Like me and Chad.

You two should switch last names—it'd be more accurate. Good thing I eventually figured that one out. A girl can only do so much homework for a guy before she starts to suspect he's using her.

I'm glad you did, and even happier you realized this guy had your name written all over him.

He's doing math. I love it when he does math.

Some features I'd definitely want in our future castle:

- Guest rooms so Mal and everyone can stay over— or move in!

- Sewing room that doesn't double as a bedroom.

- Bandstand right below the windows, so Doug can serenade me.

Oops! My glitter nail polish spilled!

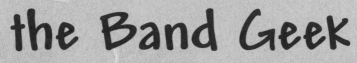
the Band Geek

Man on a Mission!

I might not be the ladies' man that Jay is but I mean, who is? If only I had his confidence with the girls. Or more specifically one girl. Ok, it's Jane. I really like Jane.

I figured maybe, just maybe, she'd go to the Cotillion with me.

Guess where I went for advice on how to ask her? That's right Jay. And let's just say he didn't really help. If he had, my smooth line would not have been, "So, do you like the carrot cake?"

Us back at the coronation.
Can you believe her moves?
Kapow!

Mal & Ben

When we met, I thought you were a chump. <u>You'd let us off the Isle.</u>

Aw, I love it when you get romantic!

Well, our evil scheme required me to get close to Fairy Godmother's wand. What better way to do that than to be your date for the coronation? A little magic made it all happen!

Yeah, but at the Coronation, we became a couple, no magic required— and nothing beats the real thing.

After that, you became king and we barely saw each other.

I hoped giving you that scooter would do the trick, but we should have just planned a holiday.

PRobably would have been less dangerous than the trip we took instead.

But then I never would have rocked that cool Isle style!

Couples who take so many pictures are actually depressed.

Earth to Ben: Your girlfriend is a fake!

the King

Carrot cake!? I'm such an idiot. Worse, it turned out she'd had pumpkin pie instead. Why in Auradon didn't I have the pie? We'd have something in common.

I tried to ask her out again after R.O.A.R. practice. Post-game analysis is that on the plus side I managed to bring up the Cotillion. Minus side: I made it look like I didn't want to go, at all.

Oh man, it was not going well.

Jane

Growing up the daughter of the school head mistress is a little like carrying stale cheese in your pocket—people tend to keep away. Worse, I was a normal kid going to school with royalty. I was resigned to being second best. Then, Mal and her gang arrived and turned everything upside down. They showed me that who you are isn't fixed, that you can change—even if nobody around you thinks it's possible.

People would accept you on the Isle. Especially if you brought that wand.

Wanna know how many times I've heard the words "Bippity boppity boo"? Trust me, you don't.

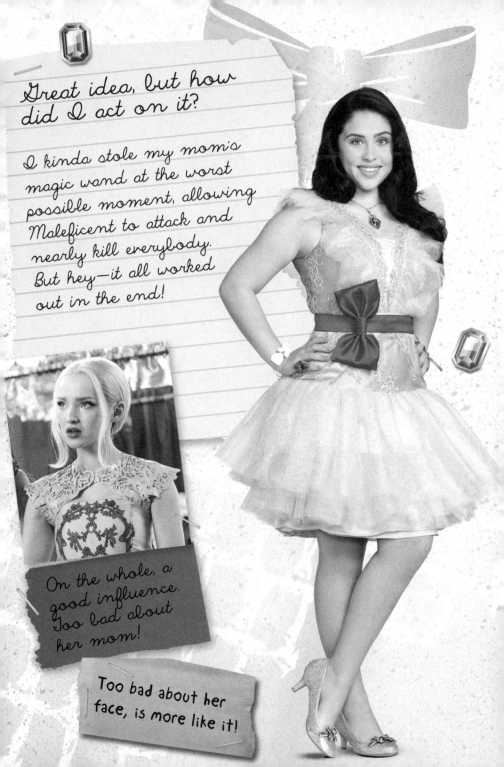

Great idea, but how did I act on it?

I kinda stole my mom's magic wand at the worst possible moment, allowing Maleficent to attack and nearly kill everybody. But hey—it all worked out in the end!

On the whole, a good influence. Too bad about her mom!

Too bad about her face, is more like it!

A LITTLE MAGIC

Wonder how I was keeping up the act of pure goodness as Ben's girlfriend? My mom's spell book! Using magic to not look like a witch. I think that's called irony.

This baby has been in my family a long time. My mother gave it to me as a going-away present. Well, going away to use it on an evil mission, that is. Still, it's like having a security blanket, though I'm pretty sure most blankets can't, you know, hypnotize people or make them fall in love.

No one likes a cheat, Mal!

✦ Love Spell ✦

Crush his heart with an iron glove
By making him a slave to love.
He'll have to eat
A sweet little treat
Made with the contents of one's soul.
Mix the following in a large iron bowl:
1 cup of butter churned by a young maiden
3/4 cup sugar
3/4 cup packed brown sugar
1 teaspoon of vanilla extract
1 tear of human sadness
2 eggs from a black hen

It was super handy when I needed to stay on top of learning all the endless customs I was expected to know.

Of course, I couldn't tell Ben about the book, only Evie knew my secret. Not that she liked me using it. But I thought I had no option, especially when I promised to cook Ben all his favorite foods. I had exactly ZERO time to do it, and believe me . . . I'm a much better witch than a cook.

A Look Back on a Dating Disaster...

Enchanted Lake

The idea was to take Mal to Enchanted Lake to make up for how busy I had been. It turned out to be a disaster.

The lunch started out well. Mal brought a whole picnic of wonderful food. She even included hor d'oevres. The date was off to a magical start!

Mal looked so perfect. Boy, was I about to learn a lesson: Your ideas of how other people **should** be sure can harm them.

When I spotted the spell book, and realized she'd used a spell to trick me, it was too much. I kinda lost it.

Released the Beast.

It got worse when I tried to use magic right there to make him forget anything had happened. Note to self: Don't do that again.

When Ben got upset, even when I tried to explain myself, I snapped, too. Everything I'd been keeping inside of me spilled out, hotter than the beef ragout.

I needed to show Ben the truth beneath the surface, so I reversed the spell. His feast became what it had really been the whole time: just a peanut butter sandwich and a cookie. Mrs. Potts I am not, and I never wanted to be. In fact, why was I even in Auradon anyway? It was clear—it was

time to leave.

Memories of My Journey Home

Went back to the dorm and put my mom in a box. Scratch that off the list of things I always wanted to do. And we were all set to go, except—I was still wearing Ben's ring. I took it off, which was hard—I mean, it was on there pretty good. Leaving wasn't so easy either.

Grabbed the scooter, chanted a travel spell—I mean, why hide my rotten ways now?—and off we went.

Me, ma, and the scooter were coming up on the barrier. I've seen birds hit this thing, and it ain't pretty. Were we gonna end up barrierkill too?

No ma'am! My mom's spell did just what it promised, and we slipped straight through. I took it as a sign I'd made the right decision.

Are you serious? Look at this thing! What a joke!

On my way over the Straight of Ursula, I remembered that I might see her daughter back on the Isle, my old enemy-slash-friend-slash-enemy. Uma... actually...

That's my name. Don't wear it out!

Straight of Ursula

The Isle

Barrier!

Landed somewhere around . . . here, and guess what? I was home.

AURADON

I can't remember looking that happy for a long time. It felt good to be bad again.

Back on the Isle

I stashed the scooter at our old hideout, and let my mom out of her box. She could go wherever she wanted, without a cage, or fittings, or Cotillion to close her in—wait, I think those last two got mixed up. Anyway we, I—I felt free for the first time in a long while.

Everything I remembered was still there. Got a hankering for some black cabbage? Or maybe you're fresh out of grime. The Isle might not have it all, but what it does have . . . smells memorable.

If I can go from Bad to Glad,

YOU CAN TOO!

A UNITED FUTURE IS POSSIBLE!
CHOOSE GOODNESS!

This poster wasn't quite capturing your facial hair. Don't worry! I fixed it!

Ever seen your face on a propaganda poster? Well neither had I, and let me tell you—it's weird.

At first I was like, "Why did they make me look like that?" And then I realized ...because that's what I look like. Sure, I'd improved my outfit, but I still had a long way to go.

Yeah, I also saw this on a wall ... it's the symbol of Uma's gang. I knew it wouldn't be long before our paths crossed.

Uma's Turf

Yeah, that IS our logo, Mal.

Think you'd be the one to give people a tour of the Isle? MY Isle? Then you're as stupid as your lizard mom. I mean that. She's so unevolved, she's barely got a brain. I could do this all day, girl.

...forgot how much the Isle stunk. I guess being Auradon made me appreciate sanitary conditions.

See this alley? You can't do anything in this alley without my permission.

Any fool knows Isle tours don't start at the grime stand, and certainly not at Mal's hideout. They start at my place, Ursula's Fish and Chips.

It's where we pirates operate from. Think it's a little soft, running a restaurant? Think again. Control food, control everything. And my gang be hangry.

Only problem—Auradon. I wanted to get my tentacles around the whole place before Mal took any more. Take it from a girl who runs a restaurant—

I hate leftovers.

MENU
frogfish
pond scur
offal
bay blob
shell sm
fish gu

Harry

Harry Hook here. I'm Uma's first mate. Uma and I met as kids at school. Favorite class: Accelerated Piracy. It was for kids with the most treacherous pirate streaks, and ours were diabolical.

If you see me, you'll see my hook—I'll make sure of it.

Funny thing happened one day when I visited Dizzy to collect some money. I ran into an old acquaintance . . . Mal!

At the sight of my hook, most people pee their pants, but Mal just stared right back at me.

So I left. Uma wouldn't have wanted me to deal with her anyway—she'd been waiting a long time to do that herself.

Glad I don't live in Bore-adon. Here on the Isle, I get to do fun things like collect money from people who owe us. Which means everyone.

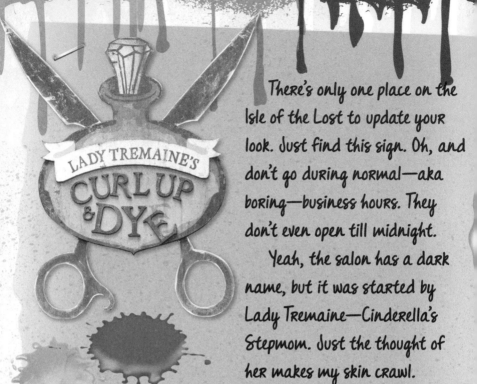

There's only one place on the Isle of the Lost to update your look. Just find this sign. Oh, and don't go during normal—aka boring—business hours. They don't even open till midnight.

Yeah, the salon has a dark name, but it was started by Lady Tremaine—Cinderella's Stepmom. Just the thought of her makes my skin crawl.

Inside looks more like a mad scientist's lab than a salon.

TRANSFORMATION

Turns out, I had a lot of things wrong. Like my nails . . .

Those soft pink nails scream, "I've fallen asleep with boredom. I might even be dead."

Then there's the dishwater blonde hair . . .

What are you? A snow queen?

They might like this in Auradon, but this girl's fire, not ice.

I told Dizzy she could go all the way, and she started getting ready. When she was done, I could barely see myself in Dizzy's broken mirror, but one thing was clear: I was back.

Want to see what I looked like?

Wave that blonde bye-bye—

purple rules!

For comparison: this washed-out doll.

What did Dizzy use for rollers? That's right: Soda cans!

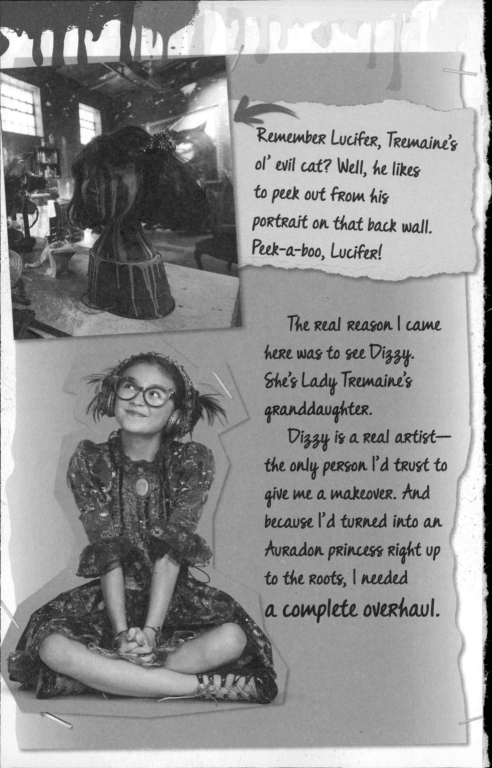

Remember Lucifer, Tremaine's ol' evil cat? Well, he likes to peek out from his portrait on that back wall. Peek-a-boo, Lucifer!

The real reason I came here was to see Dizzy. She's Lady Tremaine's granddaughter.

Dizzy is a real artist—the only person I'd trust to give me a makeover. And because I'd turned into an Auradon princess right up to the roots, I needed **a complete overhaul.**

Hey gang, what you think?

Woot! You never looked more like you.

Thought your old Isle gear was tough, but now I'm actually scared and I think I like it.

Your nails are sweet.

Thanks! Love you guys.

You look like a grape popsicle.

I paid Dizzy for the fabulous makeover and was ready to take on anything. Well, almost anything.

Riding to the Isle...in Style

The moment I found out Mal had gone, I knew I'd messed up, big time. I had to apologize, even if it meant going to the Isle of the Lost.

Evie wasn't letting me go without escorts and definitely not without a new Isle-appropriate outfit.

I figured it was too dangerous to bring Dude, and boy was he mad. He told us straight up, and you should have seen the others. It was the first time they found out he could talk!

Talk, yes. Do tricks? Forget it.

Ever since I first saw it, I'd always wanted to hot-wire the royal limo. Compared to any other car I've driven, it's like seven times as long. How would it even go around corners? Did it bend in the middle?

Ben got us through the barrier, and suddenly we were back. Being back on the Isle was odd and a little scary. Mostly because I knew Ben was totally going to give himself away.

How to Chill like a Villain

It was clear Ben really needed a lesson in flying under the radar. Without it, he was gonna blow his cover and get us all caught. We kicked up a lesson, villain-style.

It can take an intervention to change someone's ways. In this case, we were trying to correct a case of terminal goodness.

I'm not sure Ben's getting it.

Ben was kinda starting to get it. He had to dig _real_ deep to find his inner villain. Problem was, he never got past mildly unpleasant. It was only a matter of time before someone got wind of our field trip.

Gil

I'm Gil. I'm on Uma's crew. If Harry's the first mate, I'm the . . . second? Maybe there's no second. I'm just a mate, I guess.

Me and Harry have been friends since we were kids. He's a little puny compared to me, but he's got that hook to make up for it.

We started out back then, following Uma around, doing whatever she told us. It was a relief—I'm not an idea guy. I'm good with faces though, as you'll soon find out.

Uh, about me:

- My muscles are BIG.
- I like eggs. For the protein. For my muscles!
- I like showing off my cannons. (AKA my muscles.)
- Strongest man on the Isle (because of...you probably know by now).

Also, I'm not known for being a tidy eater, or tidy...anything. I'm more about strength than sophisti— How's that word end again? My dad would know— Gaston, the most amazing hunter and all-around incredible guy.

He knows **everything**.

How to Spot a Faker on the Isle

You know what's always on that ancient TV in Uma's chip shop? (When there's a signal, that is.) Auradon. Amazing Auradon, and all its celebrities. So, when Auradon's most famous person showed up here and tried to blend in, it was hard to avoid us... "fans."

My dad was somewhat obsessed with hunting the Beast. I must be a pretty good hunter too, if I caught Beast's son while just walking down the street! Of course, in the beginning he pretended to be someone else.

The 243rd
Royal Cotillion

THE EVENING'S EVENTS TO BE BROADCAST LIVE
ON AURADON ROYAL TELEVISION

BROUGHT TO YOU BY BUREAU OF ISLE AFFAIRS

These posters are annoying, but sometimes they come in handy. Even in disguise, Ben couldn't help look like that fancy king.

Here's me putting two and two together. I look so thrilled, you'd think I just found a way through the barrier. Which I guess I kinda did!

Still feel like a quiet holiday on the Isle? I wouldn't be so sure. King Ben, soon your biggest fan will know you're here . . . my captain.

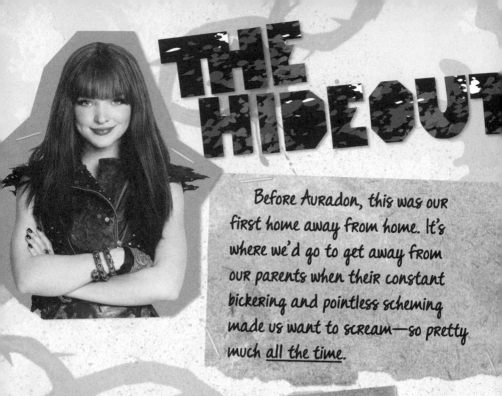

THE HIDEOUT

Before Auradon, this was our first home away from home. It's where we'd go to get away from our parents when their constant bickering and pointless scheming made us want to scream—so pretty much <u>all the time</u>.

This is my latest work. I was trying to get to the core of who we are—you know, the rotten core?

Living on the Isle is all about salvage (aka: reusing garbage), which is where we got that wood, and that old bike, and that mattress, and . . . you get the idea.

Like my thorns? They took forever, but I figure they'll scare anyone that shouldn't be here. Like a "keep out" sign but, you know, artsy-like.

A Rocky Reunion

Kind of a sad thing to put in our scrapbook, but I figure you've gotta remember the hard times—so you can learn from them. I definitely wasn't expecting Ben to show up in our lair, begging me to come back to Auradon. I just wasn't ready, but **spoiler alert:** this has a happy ending . . . eventually.

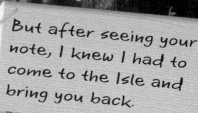

But after seeing your note, I knew I had to come to the Isle and bring you back.

I just never really felt like I belonged in Auradon. When I went back to the Isle, it felt like home so I decided to stay . . . expecting to never see you again.

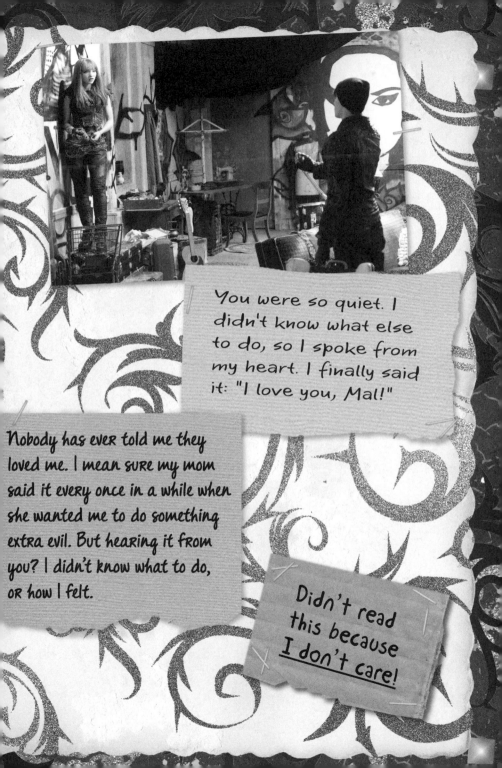

You were so quiet. I didn't know what else to do, so I spoke from my heart. I finally said it: "I love you, Mal!"

Nobody has ever told me they loved me. I mean sure my mom said it every once in a while when she wanted me to do something extra evil. But hearing it from you? I didn't know what to do, or how I felt.

Didn't read this because I don't care!

How to Handle Crisis like a Villain

First you need a crisis, and we had one as big as Maleficent <u>when she's a dragon.</u> Who knew what Uma would do to Ben?

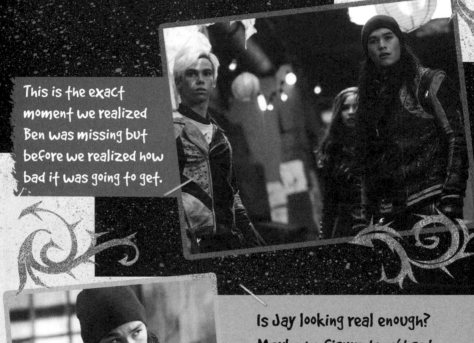

This is the exact moment we realized Ben was missing but before we realized how bad it was going to get.

Is Jay looking real enough? Maybe he figured we'd get Ben back just fine, which we did, of course. But, what it took to get him back, well, that almost made Jay lose his cool. Almost.

Look at these clown fish!

Next, you've got to figure out a plan. But before that: time for a fight. What can I say? We're villains. We're emotional.

Harry likes three things a lot: gloating, scaring people, and waving his hook around. Must have been the best day of his life.

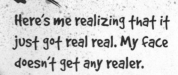

Here's me realizing that it just got real real. My face doesn't get any realer.

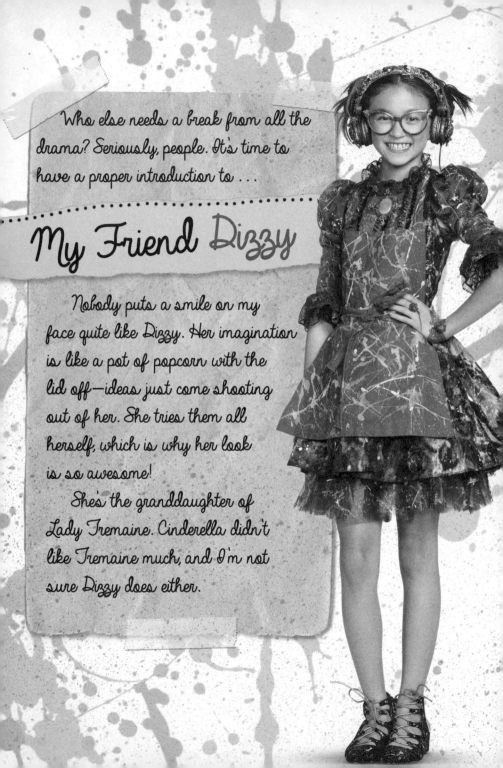

Who else needs a break from all the drama? Seriously, people. It's time to have a proper introduction to . . .

My Friend Dizzy

Nobody puts a smile on my face quite like Dizzy. Her imagination is like a pot of popcorn with the lid off—ideas just come shooting out of her. She tries them all herself, which is why her look is so awesome!

She's the granddaughter of Lady Tremaine. Cinderella didn't like Tremaine much, and I'm not sure Dizzy does either.

Dizzy's a super hard worker. I guess when your shop only opens at midnight, you have a lot of free time during the day. But when does the poor girl sleep?

She's also super supportive. She'd saved my old sketchbook and reminded me of a dress I'd made once from an old curtain. I realized it was actually inspiration from something I'd made recently for Mal.

Hair accessory? This looks like a whole 'do!

Best apron ever! When Dizzy spills dye, it ends up looking like modern art.

Imagine this one on Lonnie— amazing!

I can't decide for this one—Carlos or Jay? JK!

So pretty! Jane would love these, even more if Dizzy made them blue.

Where's the trinket for ME, Diz?

I have to admit I _really_ want this one. Those hearts jewels!

Dizzy is amazing at crafts. She made all these accessories, and gave me a bunch for the Cotillion. For someone who comes from a place full of villains, talk about being generous.

How To Almost Win An Arm Wrestle

Uma had been waiting for this since we were kids, since I dropped that bucket of rotten shrimps on her head, and named her after it. But Shrimpy wasn't going to go down without a fight. We decided to arm wrestle for Ben.

I never had a younger sister, but sometimes Dizzy makes me feel like I do. The thought of leaving her behind, again—it just didn't feel right.

She's wise beyond her years, too. She said, "You can take the girl out of the Isle, but not the Isle out of the girl." Well, I _was_ hoping there was a way I could take this girl out of the Isle.

If she were in Auradon, everyone would want her original accessories!

Arm wrestling is as much a battle of brains as it is a battle of muscle. And when you're in this stinky garbage chip shop, it's also a battle of noses. Pee-ew.

I called her Shrimpy, and almost had her beat. But then she revealed that the only thing she'd trade for Ben was Fairy Godmother's wand. It took me back to one of my worst mistakes, and if there's one thing that makes a loser, it's shame.

But I _almost_ won.

Isle Always Remember You

Sometimes "Best Friends Forever" turns out to be "Best Friends Until . . ." Was that where we were headed?

I thought I knew you so well, but somehow I didn't realize it was so hard for you in Auradon. I guess I was just so caught up loving our new home.

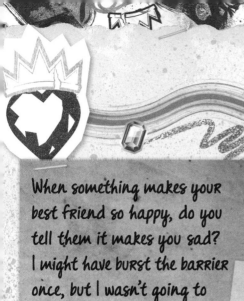

When something makes your best friend so happy, do you tell them it makes you sad? I might have burst the barrier once, but I wasn't going to do that to your bubble.

I would have stayed, you know, because you're my best friend.

If you stayed because of me, I couldn't forgive myself. And I can forgive myself for a lot.

No matter where we are, we'll be best friends until we're a couple of old ladies.

So entitled. Not everyone gets to choose where they live.

Print This!

Engineering might be a long word that takes like, an hour to say, but it'll save you in a jam. That is, if your jam happens to be making a nonmagical replica of a priceless wand to free your friend from pirates. Then it's <u>great</u>.

Step #1:

Enter your dorm to find someone already using your 3-D printer, <u>without permission</u>.

Step #2:

Kick him off the 3-D printer—without making too much fun of him for printing an action figure of himself. fragile ego?

Step #3:

Program your design, and sit tight to see what turns out—or doesn't.

Result:

Ta-da! You might think that's actually Fairy Godmother's wand Mal is holding. But it's a perfect double in every way.*

*Not actually magic.

Battle for Ben: The Trade

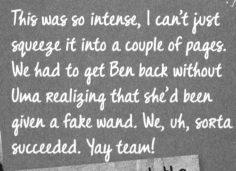

This was so intense, I can't just squeeze it into a couple of pages. We had to get Ben back without Uma realizing that she'd been given a fake wand. We, uh, sorta succeeded. Yay team!

Before you hear the lies, get the truth. Mal makes this sound like a heroic rescue. It was a swindle, straight up.

When we arrived, I thought her pirate ship would be bigger. True, her crew looked tough. But I'll take strategy over muscle any day of the week.

Mal, you've been spoiled by all those huge castles. Think I'm short on brains? In your dreams, girl.

Step I complete! I gave her the dummy wand and we got Ben back.

For now it seemed like Mal was winning. . . . But I had other tricks up my sleeve.

And then I realized that while I was practicing manners for the Cotillion, Uma was probably practicing carving my name in kittens. Things got . . . interesting. Gulp!

Battle for Ben: The Escape

Thought you were just going to walk out of here, huh? Well not till I give you a haircut...real short.

All the time Ben spent as captain of the R.O.A.R. team really paid off. His sword skills are really amazing. I think even <u>Uma</u> was impressed.

Yeah, full marks for looking good. But you want to see a lesson in swordplay? Check out my boy Gil. It looks like Carlos's cute little dog is about to need a new master.

I think even Evie's sword matches her outfit. Beautiful and deadly. How does she do it?

Rumor has it Jay is smarter than Gil. But even Gil wouldn't smile if he was about to be turned into fish food.
  Face it Mal, your crew got soft. Want proof? Your plan required a talking dog.

Luckily, we escaped from Uma's pirate gang and headed for the limo and back to Auradon.

Get over your identity crisis, Mal. It's as stale as the chip shop's Thursday night special. Wonder what that is? It's Monday and Tuesday's specials mixed together.

Dude IS a DUDE

Lots of people have dogs, and most people have a hero, but how many can say their dog is a hero? Dude totally fooled Uma! From now on, this is me at the dog park:

Other dog owner: My dog can shake a paw. What about yours?

Me: Mine can trick pirate captains into giving up prisoners. Plus, he can talk.

Someone else: ...

Seriously, Dude deserves a fan club.

Want to count the reasons why?

Maybe I'll get a pet shark. Then we'll see how tough Dude is.

1 I know, I've already said that he tricked Uma, but just a reminder: **he tricked Uma!** Do you know how smart that girl is? Try to pull the wool over her eyes, you'd be tied up in knots.

2 Might not look it, but he's extremely wise. Remember when I asked Jay for romantic advice? The best I could do was ask Jane if she liked carrot cake. Well, Dude knew what I really needed: the confidence to speak from the heart.

3 Dude's advice worked! If felt like my brain was going to melt, but I told Jane how I felt. And she agreed to go to the Cotillion with me. Look out Auradon, Carlos has a date!

All thanks to my four-legged genius.

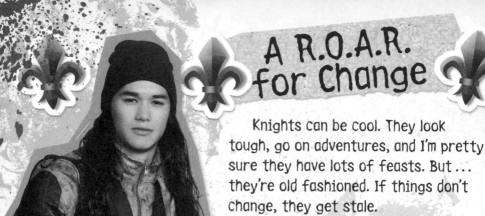

A R.O.A.R. for Change

Knights can be cool. They look tough, go on adventures, and I'm pretty sure they have lots of feasts. But... they're old fashioned. If things don't change, they get stale.

But what am I really talking about?

LONNIE. She's the opposite of stale—an air freshener. What scent? Pure Warrior Awesome. Without her, our R.O.A.R. game was going to smell like my locker right before I do laundry. Ugh.

We needed her on the team, but how? I was stumped, and then Lonnie made us bring her along to rescue Ben. This wasn't a game—we were about to face a real battle together!

It's really hitting Carlos that we are bringing Lonnie to the Isle!

Then, when we faced Uma together, I realized:
Lonnie isn't just good with a sword (she could
probably cut the whole ship in half). She's a leader.
And what do you call the leader of a team?

The rules said nothing about the captain being a man,
so technically I wasn't breaking them. And Chad reluctantly
accepted it.

But Lonnie? She was stoked. She's going to be such a
great captain, I'd trust her with my life. And guess what?
I already have.

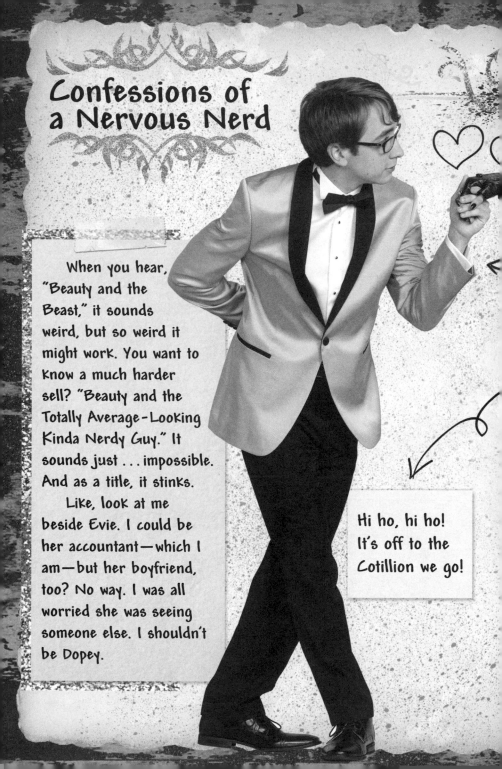

Confessions of a Nervous Nerd

When you hear, "Beauty and the Beast," it sounds weird, but so weird it might work. You want to know a much harder sell? "Beauty and the Totally Average-Looking Kinda Nerdy Guy." It sounds just . . . impossible. And as a title, it stinks.

Like, look at me beside Evie. I could be her accountant—which I am—but her boyfriend, too? No way. I was all worried she was seeing someone else. I shouldn't be Dopey.

Hi ho, hi ho! It's off to the Cotillion we go!

... and his Girlfriend!

You're cuter than Dizzy's best button.

I hate keeping secrets. But when Mal disappeared and Ben was kidnapped, I had to keep that under my tiara. I guess me being away without an explanation, well, it made Doug nervous.

There's only one boy for me, Doug. And as for princes? The last one's idea of a date was making me stand there while he talked on the phone. I'm definitely out of that market.

Get Dressed!

Every design starts out as, well, a design in my head. Since I can't show you what's going on in my head—probably a good thing, trust me—I figure I'll share the next best thing: my sketches.

Here are sketches from my old sketchbook from the Isle. Blank paper is hard to find, so I used old newspapers. Who says villains can't be good recyclers?

I know, I was pretty pleased, too. And I wasn't the only one looking fantastic.

Mal was right. Talking to the press can give a girl butterflies! Good thing Doug was there, looking so sharp he could cut diamonds.

You could mistake Lonnie for a princess, even though a day before she was battling pirates with a sword in her hand. Talk about a fashionable fighter.

I don't think I'll ever let Jay go back to his tough guy style. He just looks too good when he dresses up. Look out, ladies!

These are newer and done on grade-A (A for Auradon) blank sheets. I miss not seeing ads for the Curl Up & Dye right beside my drawings, but I definitely feel more professional.

Recognize this guy? Having friends who are into experimenting with their style is amazing!

As much as I love designing for my friends, it's only fair that I make a few things for me, too. I wanted to go all-out dramatic for the Cotillion.

Want to see how it ended up?

All my other designs were really just practice for Mal's dress. Making it feel right took a few adjustments, but in the end, she looked amazing.

Y'all looked pretty good ... before I slithered in and broke up the party!

Pirate Princess

On the Isle, we dream big—it's not like we have many entertainment options. Want to know my dream? Well, you're looking at it.

I've never owned a fancy dress, never been able to afford one. But walking down those stairs like royalty, it was like I'd been wearing that dress my whole life.

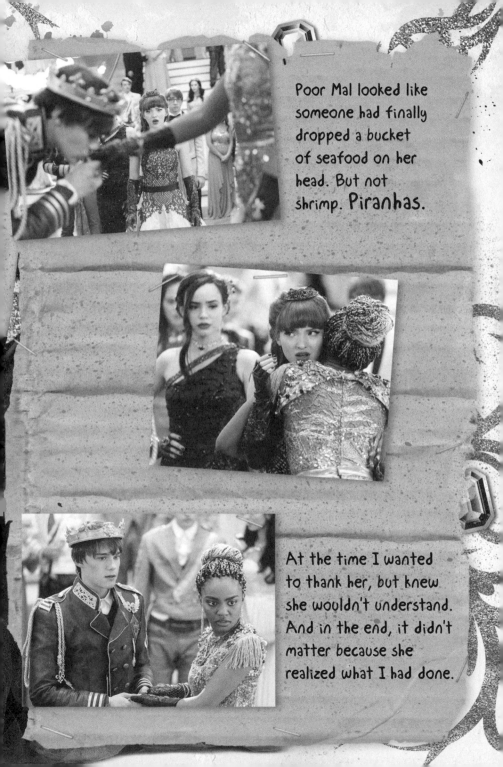

Poor Mal looked like someone had finally dropped a bucket of seafood on her head. But not shrimp. Piranhas.

At the time I wanted to thank her, but knew she wouldn't understand. And in the end, it didn't matter because she realized what I had done.

True Love?

The Cotillion was going great . . . until my boyfriend professed his love to my biggest enemy. To make it worse, I was surrounded by beautiful stained glass images of couples whose love changed the world.

Aurora and Prince Philip. They had to fight against my own mom to be together. That's serious because trust me, she fights dirty. And their kiss? Strong enough to break <u>even her magic.</u>

Jasmine and Aladdin. Insecure about telling Jasmine he lived on the street, Aladdin pretended to be a prince. Wow, could I ever relate. When Jasmine found out the truth, she loved him even more.

Then maybe the most amazing of all, Belle and Beast. They couldn't seem more opposite. But, their connection was so powerful it showed each of them <u>who they might become</u>. Wow.

I'm a villain, he's royalty, so maybe we were a bit like that. Opposites. Then I saw the stained glass that Ben had made of us.

The moment I saw it, I knew. Ben really loved me. He wanted to help me grow in ways I'd been too scared to try. In this world, <u>that's as true as love gets</u>.

I also know Ben couldn't love Uma. Evie and I figured out she must have found my spell book and used it on Ben. Breaking the spell would take a very special kiss. But would ours be as strong as Sleeping Beauty's?

When Uma's plan fell apart, she still tried to get the wand. That's when I let my "inner dragon" out. When the fight was over, I was able to show Ben my true self. Purple always was my favorite color.

The Future Starts NOW

Maybe it was just wearing two stunning gowns in one night, but I was feeling inspired. There's no limit to what we can do, if we do it together.

My only regret is that Dude didn't come. Anyway, I'm not sure he can dance a two-step.

I'm relieved we didn't need our swords because mine doesn't go with this outfit.

The Cotillion didn't go how I planned—it was better! The best part was being your date, Carlos.

Me, too. Though I'm pretty sure you could make a sword look good with anything, captain.

Once upon a time, four Villain Kids came to Auradon. Auradon was never the same again, and neither were we.

And that's our scrapbook!

If we didn't have each other, I don't think there'd be much of us or Auradon left intact.

Yeah, wow—things got even more insane than I thought they had. But I guess when you add pirates and magic to the mix, anything can happen.

I hope it's not the last we see of Uma. As long as she keeps her hands off my boyfriend, I think we could be friends one day. Or at least . . . less enemies?

Right, girl? Maybe. But I'll always be your pirate queen.

What shall we do with all this space?
Maybe you should add some memories
of your own. C'mon, don't hold back!

Why thank you Mal, so very kind. Maybe
you're not totally terrible, old friend, just
99%. When you're in your palace, think of
me. I'll be on the Isle, back in the chip shop,
slinging the Tuesday special, still dreaming
of a way to get off this rock.

We might not agree on
much, but we do on this:
You haven't heard the last of me.

His Royal Majesty,
King Ben of Auradon,
and his Councilor Ms. Evie of the Isle
hereby request the pleasure of
your company, Dizzy Tremaine,
for the current academic year at
Auradon Prep. Please notify
his Majesty's couriers of your
response to this Request.

We'd love you to join us
at Auradon Prep
Will you come?

King Ben

What?! Can you
believe this?
That's a pretty easy
question to answer...

YES!

Image Credits:
Photographs courtesy of Shutterstock.com:
p.1: background paper texture: David M. Schrader, foreground paper: 7th Son Studio;
tape: Marie Smolej; p. 12: handwritten doodles: vector graphics designed by Freepik;
p. 13: paper: Dawid Lech; Gatefold 2, back: tape: Marie Smolej;
p. 20: paper: David M. Schrader; p. 26: paper: R-studio; p; 30: music: olenadesign;
p. 36: R-studio; p. 42: paper: Gordan; Gatefold 5, front: makeup: Picsfive,
paint splatter: Milan M; p. 55: paper: TADDEUS

Studio Fun International
An imprint of Printers Row Publishing Group
A division of Readerlink Distribution Services, LLC
10350 Barnes Canyon Road, Suite 100, San Diego, CA 92121
www.studiofun.com

Written by Charlie Blake

Studio Fun International is a registered trademark of
Readerlink Distribution Services, LLC.
All notations of errors or omissions should be addressed to Studio Fun International,
Editorial Department, at the above address.

ISBN: 978-0-7944-3955-2

Manufactured, printed, and assembled in Stevens Point, Wisconsin, U.S.A. WOR/08/17
21 20 19 18 17 1 2 3 4 5